I0779973

BOOKS & SMITH
New York Editors

LIFE AND ITS TIMES

Rafael Antonio Tejada

Translated from the Spanish by Edgar Smith.

A Books&Smith Publication.

Winner of an accessit at
the Federico García Godoy
Funglode Awards/GFDD 2014.

Memory is a key
that opens doors
towards the past.
These allow us entry
to the very center
—where it is still the present.

Rafael Antonio Tejada

To Lidia Marcelina Monegro
—for the stories told
and the magic in her voice.
To Juana Carolina, Isael, and Arián
—for accepting the continuation of the act.

Words about the book

Life and its times is a journey through the experiences of characters who, through their dialogues, describe themselves, and at the same time tell us about others.

It also recreates lives that take place in different times, to which in some way we are linked, either by reference or directly.

In the actions of these characters, in the worlds or stories that interconnect to tell the central story, love manifests itself as a big force. A force capable of overcoming otherness to allow life to its fullest.

Dinorah Coronado,
author of *La mujer del bodeguero*.

Despite having made a name for himself as a poet in what most people refer to as the Dominican Diaspora (whose "headquarters", at least literature-wise, appears to be New York), Rafael Tejada introduced himself to me as a narrator, a storyteller of sorts. Not literally, no, but in the best way a man of letters can be introduced to anyone: through a book he titled *La sed del metal* (*The Thirst of Metal*), a collection of short stories that effectively precluded everything I would later read and admire in his work. If I were forced to pinpoint a single remarkable aspect of Rafael's style, I would have to choose his unmatched serious approach towards literature in general. This is a hardworking writer who takes his craft with profound seriousness. There are no shortcuts here and not a hint that something has been left to chance. Every word has significance. Every phrase chosen with care. I enjoy this angle because the degree of commitment that permeates these pages speaks volumes on the character of the author and his self-demand of greatness.

Edgar Smith,
translator of *Fiptisio '89* and *A Treatise on Absence*.

Chapter One

The flight of the swallows

I'm almost rid of stress. I have been depositing it over there, on the other side. Off the beach. Where the prostitutes, hair-braid weavers, improvised musicians, scammers, and the dog that almost bit me wander about.

I'm almost there. Almost. This pier-style terrace, which rises and runs from the sands to the depth, evokes worlds. The creaking of wood under my feet reveals times that lurk. Two swallows slice the air in their play.

In the distance, the presence of a huge ship halts one's gaze. A plane taking flight from Las Americas airport plays the game of rediscovering motion.

Fernando talks to me. He says something that I can't quite catch. The waters dance and through them I discover the shapes of the air.

"Boca_Chica," I say, as if trying to convince myself that this is all real.

The ship moves away. Little by little, quite slowly, it gains distance —opening the sea and, somehow, getting closer to the past. To that past where I imagine Luis hiding in another ship just as imposing. Luis moves around, crouching, hiding, going from one spot to the next. Between containers, he looks for a place to protect himself from the sun and hide from the navy officers—they will probably come around to check before the ship reaches high sea.

If everything goes well, in just a few days, he will be touching dry land in the United States of America, Panama, or somewhere else. It doesn't matter where. Now the only urgency, the essential thing for Luis is to leave the country.

All the stories I heard about "El Regina" sped through my mind like fugitive birds on the run. Yet, as you will notice, one of them stayed behind—lurking in the surroundings.

*****

It was six o'clock in the evening. From the radio, Sonia Silvestre's voice was soothing, just as a friend's voice would. The song seemed to stir the moment.

"The afternoon is crying, and it is because of you..."

Leonides heard the phrase. Like a bird in a frenzied flight, it invaded the moment, pierced her deeply, so deeply that on its way back, after having coursed through her entire being, as it was leaving to make way for another

16

phrase, it brought tears with it.

The young woman cried for the life and death of her Luis. She wept for what was and for what could have been that part of her life —that should have belonged to them both.

She stood up —all doubt left behind on the beat-up sofa. She walked to the mirror and envisioned her soul going through a new path. Behind lay a life that was dying, like those worlds that fall into the abyss in their unconscious pursuit of the sun—around six o'clock, just before the arrival of shadows. Once again, Sonia —her voice like a sword, slashing though the thickness of silence:

"The evening grew sad along with me, and I need that evening to cover me."

She opened a drawer, grabbed her hair up, and, like someone who wants to tame a wild animal, tied it tightly. She then took the scissors out and cut it without mercy or hesitation. Her mind was made up: she would become a nun.

We all set sails together, so to say. The Regina took a part of Leonides's life with it. And a bit of our lives, too —those of us who attest to her time. I don't know why but the truth is the death of someone we know almost always plunges us into a lethargy from which it is only possible to leave gradually.

This happened to us with Luis and everything we wanted to know back then —all the questions in the air: 'Why didn't he trust her?' 'Why didn't he tell her he would stow away in the Regina?' And how, once there, did he allow himself to be convinced of entering that sealed water tank?' 'What was his death like?' These questions never knew any answers but stayed close by... waiting.

To speak about El Regina is to bring back the medley of stories that comprise the central narrative of one of the greatest tragedies occurred in this land—so used to forgetting.

We never imagined that this ship, with Panamanian license and flag, which once or twice a year kissed the port of the Ozama River, would become the stage for images that would forever pierce our souls like daggers. From it, death spread out to all corners of the country. There were many reasons driving those who desperately tried to leave the island: political and financial, mostly. For others, it was even more complicated than that.

In short, any reason was good enough to quench the thirst of exile that always pursues an islander. Whatever their motives, they did not deserve such fate. A handful of soulless men, after charging over twenty people thousands of dollars to stowaway in the ship, locked them in a water tank with no ventilation and let them die of asphyxia. Only a few survived.

Children, women, men... we all experienced the pain. Some directly and others through the emotion in the voice of the *Radio Guarachita*[1] announcer:

---

[1] One of the very first and most popular radio stations in the Dominican Republic.

"Good afternoon, if we can call it that. This time, misfortune has chosen us. Today we suffer the pain of the mother, the father, the brother, the sister, the girlfriend... the wife who will no longer see their loved one. Beyond the horizon; far away, after drinking the waters and their salts with our eyes, the travelers of the Regina disappear. Now we see them in the thirsty embrace of another embrace. In the orphaned spaces, in the weeping of the mothers; we can see them on the dock. In time their desires wander. Endless journey is their odyssey. A dagger that constantly wounds in memory. We can see them. We will always see them. They will return, waving their songs of absence; they will make themselves present behind the Alcazar. Facing the Ozama River, the stowaways of the Regina sail dreams."

There was an emphasis in his words. Something that compelled us to tears.

The Regina was a huge ship. Big in size and hope. Some sort of Dominican Titanic. It was so famous that its image outgrew the port to cover the entire national territory. It was like one of those tropical systems that start with barely a cloud and end up drenching every single thing in its path —as if offering soaked gifts whose mud scent stays with us for good. This is how The Regina stamped itself in our memories. It was all anyone talked about. Before and after the tragedy, we saw people we weren't used to seeing. They came with different tasks, but in the end, they ended up doing the same thing: planting the seed of their individual fame in every dialogue, in every attempt to stir enthusiasm among potential travelers, or to show solidarity with the pain of those close to the victims. A seed that germinated and then grew to the size it holds today.

"They are planning a trip. It's safe… and it's happening. For a mere two thousand dollars they'll take you; no need to get any papers. They pick you up and put you on El Regina, that's the name of the ship, and you do not have to worry about the authorities; they are in on it," proposed the first ones, the sellers of hope.

And then the others came at the time of tears:

"We are sorry. It is a tragedy to lose someone so young and hard-working as your son. We pray for your comfort and strength, and urge you to trust God's mysterious ways."

We heard this same speech repeated so many times that we ended up solidifying it, as if it were malleable matter that we could transform from one state to another. We made it concrete. Now we see it in the shape of cement crosses everywhere. That was one of the ways we found to relieve ourselves of all that weight. Sometimes I think we were like a dam that gradually accumulated the water flowing in from other points until it reached its limit. That's why we opened the valves of our eyes and let out those waters that were drowning us inside.

A long time passed before Leonides felt that the whirlwind created by Luis's death had come to an end. She had overcome it. She knew this because now she could look back and remember all and every single thing without getting heart-crushed. It had not been like this at the beginning. To reach this state of mind, she had had to overcome the feelings that took away the vitality from her hours. She fought hard against her sadness.

She reflected on the origin of this feeling now hovering over her path. She searched for it and realized that the answer would not be deciphered in any simple way. Not in one fell swoop. No. What she was experiencing had a complex origin. She knew it.

In addition to the regret of believing she had been fooled, there were the doubts. She didn't know if, at the time of the decision, she had been present in Luis's thoughts. If, upon returning from his trip, he had thought he would be returning to her or, on the contrary, she had been but a fling to him.

On the other hand, she understood that she had not been sincere enough with him —or with herself. She silenced the call of desire when it had screamed to be heard.

"No."

"Why not?"

"Because it's only a few days left. It's better this way, you know it."

"No, I don't know," he said as he rubbed both of his hands along her thighs.

"How can you do that? You want them to see us?" She complained after looking around in a circle and noticing that, just like them, others were still hanging around in the park.

"No. Just stop the crap and love me more," he said.

She got scared. She realized that the effect of his words was stronger than what she had felt from his hands the minute before. She decided to entrench herself.

"Let's go!"

And they left. But in her mind, from that moment on, the world was moving at the speed of those rubbing fingers. Days later, the radio brought the news like sharpened knives:

"We count the casualties in the dozens. They are being deposited on the shores of the Ozama river, across from the Alcazar. We ask that, if there's someone in your family you have not seen for a while, someone you were starting to worry about, come over. You might have to identify them among the corpses."

Then the shock, the unequivocal reality: Luis among the dead, denying all possibilities of them becoming plural; leaving her to perpetuate her state of singular. There were no doubts left in her, as previously stated, she had decided to become a nun. That was the way to go: according to her possibilities, the only viable solution. Before, she had plunged into what had been lived; like a hungry cat, she had explored the surroundings of her past. She tenaciously searched its corners for something to cling to. Something that offered the opportunity to latch herself onto her habitual world. But it was useless. Everything moved towards a different time; and she was left outside with the certainty of needing to belong to someone or somewhere. To what had been, she could only access through her memories.

*****

Fernando speaks to me again. He brings me back to his time.

"I want you to write about me, so that they remember me when I am gone," he says. In his words, an air of a farewell that is not immediate.

I have never narrated anything that exceeds the space of six pages, and no one had ever suggested that I do it. This is why when he asked me to write his memoirs, I was a bit perturbed. A strange feeling took hold of me, and I thought that something similar must happen to someone who has been kidnapped. He or she is a prisoner until the ransom is paid. In my case, I knew that I would only be free when I fulfilled my task.

"I would like you to write about my life. I don't want to die without seeing that book about us. I don't want to," he reiterated.

Fernando is my younger brother. He landed on my reality to share life and its times. To jump with me from the boulder to the river, from one branch to the other, from crying to laughter, from childhood to the present and vice versa. Now he is at war: Cancer. They have told him that the tumor removed from his brain is carcinogenic, so he is at war. Day in and day out, he fights against this evil.

"You know, Nando, I am in favor of the plural. I think individuality is a failed attempt to walk away from ourselves. My life is made up of shared experiences. Every look, every smile, every cry and joy belong to us, and at the same time, to the others. This is why, to write about you, I would have to write about myself, about the people who populate our worlds, and about the times that belong to the time in which our names wander. Do you agree?"

"Of course; there are so many memories that I would like to keep forever. Remember the bower?"

"Yes, yes, I remember. I remember the columns supporting the roof. They reached so high, as if trying to look over the trees."

"Yeah, I heard grandpa say once, 'Solid wood. Those sticks come from trees cut down at their strongest—when mature. That is why they are so hard. Woodworms cannot eat through them.'"

"I remember there was on each post some decoration or hanging plant that made the vision of the straight line softer towards the top. And up there, like brakes stopping the eyes, the cane-woven roof. We enjoyed staring at this ocher sky that seemed like a universe. Through its tiny crevices and cracks, we discovered hidden worlds. Do you remember?"

A spider travels horizontally from east to west; then vertically, in a direction that seems south to north. Then, in a circular motion, from the outside in. One, two... many routes, until it gets closer to the center. The circular trip shorter and shorter. It is now at rest. Once the work is done, it is time for the reward. Some stranger shall fall into the trap the way my eyes fell onto the splendor of the flower that, at that moment, the hummingbird kissed. There were peonies and begonias: timid pinks, intense yellows and purples.

'Chila takes very good care of her flowers. After shouting and scolding, that's what she does best,' Grandpa said once, denoting in his words a distaste already tamed.

The bower was part of our daily life. It belonged to the house, but it was spaced about ten meters apart. Like the warehouse shaft and the kitchen, it had its own status. It was like a connection among all the spaces and the people who inhabited them: The laborers, the women of the house, the grand-parents, and us, who played a game of catching dreams in the eyes of one or another daytime dreamer. Leonides was quite the woman already, and Zunilda was entering the age in which the world had started to wake up in her being. I remember it well.

"What about Mapenga? You do remember old Mapenga, don't you? Fernando asked.

"Of course, how could I not! Whenever he came around, the sun had not yet finished climbing up the morning hours…

'Hello, hello, Chila. How you doing over here?'

'Hello, Mapenga. We're fine. How you doing?'

'It's going for me. It's the Álvarez who have it rough; poor people, it's one bad thing or another. I'm coming from over there now, and I can tell you: they all down with sorrow. Evil has befallen them. Only God knows why He's allowed it. They say the eldest son is a Communist, and that's why them police took him, and they won't let no one see him.'

'Jesus, Mary, and Joseph! Poor boy! Oh, what he must be going through. May God protect him!'

'Amen. Yet what I'm telling you, it is true. They not doing well, no, no.'

'Hey, Mapenga, tie that horse over there, farther that way. I don't want it making a mess over here. You can clean and clean again, but the smell of that beast always stays on the soil.'

'No, Chila, no worries; my horse won't do nothing like that.'

'I hear you, but tie it far away, please; and then let's see what you brought. I hope it is something good this time because what you brought the other day, aside for the flute we bought for the boys, I tell you, the other day, it was pure trifle.'

'Sure, yeah, Chila; for sure, yeah. Today I brought you the good stuff.'

'Leonides, bring Mapenga a cup of coffee.'

'No, Chila, thank you very much; I prefer a glass of that sweet lemonade that you know how to make so good. Because of the heat, you know.'

'Bring him the lemonade, and add another plate to the table. This one won't leave until he's eaten,' said grandma."

Mapenga was a corpulent man. His skin, although sun-burned, was quite light. We never knew his real name and never bothered to ask. Some names are just not necessary. Furthermore, it seems to me that Mapenga was the one word that went well with his prominent belly, and the saddlebags that he always carried on his horse. It suited his personality perfectly. It was like a kind of encompassing synonym for an array of conflicting terms: obese, nice, ugly, good-natured and traveler. These were some of the concepts that, added together, resulted in the feeling of his presence.

"Rafa, are you OK?"

"Yes, for a second there, I felt like I was back in that moment. Some experiences feel so close."

"Hell, yeah. Some times just linger."

"Yes, true that. There are times that go beyond the spheres that measure it. Times whose seconds are dressed in the laughter and cries of vertical lives; in the vision of beings that, by the mere fact of coinciding with us, belong to us; and they make our existence part of theirs," I thought out loud.

"And what about Cuica and Cedazo?"

"Cuica and Cedazo? Oh, my God, so many things!" Fernando laughs.

For the first time I see him laugh, and it makes me sad. His laughter is an echo of a time when death was afraid of us.

"Yeah, those two."

"Oh, those were two crazy women!"

"That is not entirely true. And even if it were, that would not disqualify them as potential characters for our story."

"I agree," he added, and we paused the dialogue.

In the first days, it did not go too well for Cuica and Cedazo in their journey through our world. As with everyone who has ever started a conquest, they were rejected; and more than one story was made up in their names. I remember we used to say they were witches and stole children — they shrunk them and hid them in the saddlebags they always carried hanging from their shoulders and under their arms. Thus, under that aura, we saw them on one of those afternoons that they came to the house.

Grandpa had told them they could come. And so, it was. Since then, twice a week, the two women would show up, and without a word from anybody, they took hold of the broom and swept up and down all the way from the entrance to the most remote corners, at the far end of the patio. Fernando and I watched them from the bower; and if they ever came even a bit closer, we always fled as fast as hummingbirds.

They're not taking me, I repeated to myself several times, always keeping my distance.

The names of Cuica and Cedazo did justice to their habit of picking up everything they found in their path. Cuica, the mother, always went in front. She collected the things that were important to her, and if anything was out of reach, Cedazo was there to complete the action.

These two women led a truly strange life. And although at that time we did not know where they lived for sure, we knew about their constant wanderings, thanks mainly to the stories they themselves told about the places they had visited. Just like Mapenga, they were a source of information about witnessed events in recent times.

Chapter Two

Vero's days

In those days, attracted by the Amapola trees, the Cundeamores appeared in our lives. This was not their real last name, though. We dressed them up with this nickname sometime after their arrival. And that was due to the ease with which they showed affection to one another. No one ever saw them angry. They kissed and hugged often—and at the least expected moments.

Ramos, I remember, was their last name. Their job was cutting and carving Amapola trees for wood. The father, Emiliano Ramos, and Luis, the son, had an extraordinary resemblance. Carmen, the mother, was a woman of affable character. She had soft facial lines and straight black hair. Her laugh was a song naturally integrated into the

sounds of the forest, and I must say that in more than
one occasion it served as a guide for me to know the
right pathway to Vero.

Vero was their daughter —a beautiful girl.
Both Luis and she arrived to embed themselves in
our worlds and never leave it again.

The afternoon cried the redness of the poppies. When the time came, falling was inevitable for
the flowers up there, and they did so like drops of
water in a rain of petals that covered the entire
ground with its splendor. The sun was planted in the
middle of the sky on that spring day. A soft breeze
all around us, and I think it was one of its currents
that brought us the Cundeamores. I saw them arrive
on the road and immediately suspected an irrever-
sible change in our lives. Two horses pulled a large
wagon that looked like a house in motion. Emiliano
got off and, after speaking with grandpa, obtained
the permission he required, and went toward the
coffee plantations —toward where the tall Amapola
trees grew. My eyes chased after the newcomers;
and for the first time they kissed the cheeks of the girl
who, from the back of the cart, seemed to extend me
an invitation.

"And now, what are you thinking about?"

"Everything, Fernando. I continue to walk
the paths of our lives. Revisiting instances. I am not
quite done remembering an event when the next
one comes knocking as if they were fighting one
another to be part of that story you want me to write

about. Just now, for instance, my mind was with the Cundeamores."

"With Vero, you mean."

"Yes, with Vero… with Luis and Leonides; and everyone who interacted with us back then.

"Do you remember? In the afternoons we went deep in the forest. From the ground, we collected the sound of our footsteps over the dead leaves on our way to the camp. As we have said, since their arrival, the Cundeamores transformed our environment. What had been previously a known array of coffee, cocoa and tall Amapola trees, had now reinvented itself as a world of new experiences."

"Yes, it's true; at first they were like half savages. What with sleeping up in the hills, in a hut covered with branches for a roof and no bed, well..." Fernando said, an indecipherable grin on his face.

"They were more in contact with nature; that's true. I remember that first impression. But only at the beginning, because later they became a part of us and shared with us: the school, their time, life… and the protests."

"The protests, yes; gee, so much running! The commotions between the guards and the students: those guards did not play. And you, man, you really liked Vero!"

"We were just children. I liked running with her when she ran; and my heart skipped a beat every time I saw her. She was a beautiful girl."

"Yes, but before the accident, because after..."

"Later, not so much. But I like to remember her as she was before; what happened... it was so sad—like a thorn hurting her past."

"Don't beat yourself up. It was not your fault."

"Yes, I know. I was there, though, at that moment; and I know that, out of all her memories of me, that's the one she remembers the most.

I remember she was running. I ran after her. In the surroundings, behind the trees, and back along the same route to the campfire.

'Look, my mom is boiling the clothes[2]!' She called.

'Yeah, I know. Just don't get too close; you could get burned,' I said.

'No, I won't burn, look!'

She rushed closer to the pitcher atop the stones that served as fireplace, and my eyes saw how she touched the already hot container, and how, in pain, she dropped to the ground. As she fell, her left leg kicked the stones, tipping the pitcher over. I saw the boiling water fall on her body. My eyes captured the horrible images of that moment that grew into an indelible memory."

"I was there, too. I just don't blame myself.

---

[2] Housewives used to 'boil clothes' as a washing technic. They would do it by riverbanks for easier access to water and on improvised fireplaces made of wood-sticks and stones.

This is life; or are you going to blame yourself too when I die for having been with me in certain moments of my life?"

"*Coño*, Fernando. Don't say things like that," I recriminated. Then we went silent again.

*****

Leonides came with us that time with the excuse of seeing Vero. And we saw her. Luis was there. Vero's burns had not yet healed. We knew it because her body was still covered with the juice and crushed leaves of the Sauco tree, and because of Juana's subsequent comment:

'She's almost healed. Thank God, things weren't that serious.'

'Thank God,' Leonides said. Then, unconsciously, her eyes searched for Luis's. He allowed the embrace of their glances.

The weather became rough —as if the love that arose between Luis and Leonides was rained over with sheer strength. And the Guaraguao[3] arrived too with their protest songs:

'How sad my people live on cardboard roofs! What

---

3 Los Guaraguao (Est. 1973) is a Venezuelan musical group framed within what was considered then 'the new Latin American song movement.'

is happening in the world, in humanity, that today's young people cannot live in peace? Answer me, Uncle Juan, don't stay silent on me. Please answer if there is no reason for us to keep fighting.'

A call it was, this song —a call and a rude awakening for the young.

Suddenly, their hands were adorned with books. Like messenger doves they had brought along knowledge. Arguments on Marxism, Capitalism, and the Proletariat, or debates about Social Classes were a common thing of that time.

'Sartre said: 'Man is condemned to be free.'
'That's a good quote.' Luis said.
'Yes, it is. It makes me wonder, how can someone be persecuted just for reading these things?' Leonides asked.
'I don't know, but I think what we are experiencing is an injustice. Even I go hiding when they say the guards are coming. I go up to the mounts and hills. I run into the other boys up there.'
'They call them Socialists, which, for the guards, is the same as criminals. And, the truth is, I don't see what's wrong with them. On the contrary, they are like you and me. They want things to be different —they want equality, that's all.'
'The other day a fellow by the name of

Valerio Álvarez, that was his name, came by. He was in a hurry, going, as they say, 'like the devil's slingshot'. He stopped at some point, desperate as he seemed, and asked for a glass of water. My mother gave it to him. He drank as if he wanted to put out a fire inside of him. Before he left, he thanked her and then screamed his own name at the top of his lungs, as if to ensure that we would not forget it, as though he knew that we would soon see him again. He dropped this book.'

'Great book. They only read things that feed their brains.'

'They are not as bad as the guards say.'

'No, they are not. The problem is that those in power do not want the poor to claim their rights. Even the priests are saying the rich have forgotten about God. Jesus preached equality among all, and that's what the boys ask for, that resources be managed in a better way.'

'We agree on that.'

'Wouldn't it be dangerous to keep this book?'

'Maybe, yeah, but we are going to take care of ourselves; no one should know that we have it.'

This is how Luis ended the dialogue. He tried not to grant any more importance to the matter. However, within the perimeter of their stillness, like flies, their very first fears had already settled.

Chapter Three

Zunilda

Zunilda must have been the most beautiful woman in the entire region. I remember her long hair, her silhouette with curves that insinuated themselves through the thin fabrics that often hugged her body. I remember her gaze, faint and vague, from eyes in whose brown color one could read the climax of innocence. A young woman, at the age of seventeen, with a body that denoted the ripeness of a fruit ready to be tasted. Zunilda ignored that she was desired, but the truth was that, by then, her presence was already nestled in the corners of more than one of the local men's world of desire. That, of course, included Dionisio Mercado.

The boy had an athletic build to him. His light skin turned reddish every time the sun came over him. She liked him, but he also awoke in her a feeling that shifted between innocent desire and fear.

A mix of emotions that made her daydream and give up at the same time. Each of his muscles and facial traits suited his physique, yet all the stories she heard about him made her feel bad and were reason enough to reject him.

'A *tíguere*[4]… that man is a *tíguere*,' all the mothers said. At night, his name invaded their daughters' thoughts as they prayed, 'From wretched men, deliver us, oh Dear Lord.'

At the age of eighteen, Dionisio decided that he did not need any more schooling. On the contrary, everything he wanted to know, life would teach him. Since then, he committed himself to working the land and, according to him, to the good life. Soon after, friends, alcohol and women came along.

The first to taste the alcohol-reddened color of his eyes was Fiordaliza, the girl who helped his mother with the kitchen chores. Their first carnal encounter occurred in a sudden. They were alone. He looked at her. She looked at him the same way she always looked at him—with repressed desire. He looked at her one more time and, before they knew it, they were already on the ground, moving and moaning, like dry leaves shaken by the breeze. After her, there came Vivian and then Mercedes. All

---

[4] *Tíguere* is Dominican slang for thug, a street-savvy man or a hoodlum.

short-term love affairs, because he defined himself as a free man, "a man not tied to any woman." This he believed until the day he started to suspect otherwise.

It was springtime. The flowers came from within the bushes. They opened up and let the sun kiss them and let us fill them up with our eyes. The butterflies drew loopholes in the air and landed then anywhere, as if intent on spreading out the miracle of color. Zunilda was hunting butterflies. Dressed in a white-pink dress, she gave the impression of being Alice, escaped from the park in her fantastic world, and that our world was, too, a world of wonders. Nevertheless, as real as we were, we knew that her encounters would not be with giant rabbits nor with characters made of cards but with fellow humans of flesh and bone—as real as time itself.

Everything was in an uproar. The wind beat the leaves of the ferns and they, in a chlorophyllic dance, covered everything in light and dark shades of green. The tension was of incalculable proportions, as if the road foresaw the fortuitous encounter between the sexes. Dionisio was approaching from the opposite side. For some time now, he had felt the urgent need to expel the liquid that had accumulated in his bladder. He felt that he could not hold it anymore. He stopped, got off his horse, looked around, and, when he saw no one approaching, took for granted the consummation of the act. He positioned himself for the unload. However, this part of the road was a bend that, in about similar percentages, opened up for either privacy or surprise.

He gave in to the unburdening—closing his eyes for a moment. When he opened them, it was a shock to discover the most beautiful reality: Zunilda was there —standing just a few meters away. With her blond hair, olive-green eyes, and an expression that mixed fear and surprise and ran from her head to her toes. She stared at him not knowing what to do. For another second she stood there. She then ran as one who has seen the devil in the flesh. He climbed back on his horse and resumed his journey. They went separate routes into the distance, but parts of that moment left with each one—and they had the suspicion that this would not be their last encounter.

The sculpture of the Virgin of Fátima is the very representation of purity. Her white attire speaks of an immaculate, clean, sinless being. For this reason, the girl to represent her had to possess shapes and expressions similar to those of the saint—Furthermore, a healthy soul, free of impurities. They all agreed that the young woman possessed these qualities and, for the current year then, she must be the one to bear such honor.

The day came. Dressed in white, with the crown of the virgin covering her head, and surrounded by lilies, Zunilda radiated peace. Everyone looked at her and praised how well she represented the saint. She looked towards the crowd. Her heart was in joy. She had always wanted to be the image of Fátima; so much so that now she felt divine, and even came to believe that, through her, the virgin could work miracles.

Her eyes were fixed on the crowd—they seemed to spread away their brown, almost honey color. She looked on and, at the same time, gathered new images. With them, she was trying to erase the one she had picked up back at the bend in the road—the only stain in her caste-full world.

Dionisio was there, too. He didn't feel like a saint or a devil. He had come because he wanted to see again that contrast of white-pink and brown on Zunilda's face. He didn't know how, but the truth was, since their last encounter, the girl's presence had asked for asylum in his life and he had conceded it.

*****

The first news of Dionisio's interest in Zunilda was given to her Grandma through a Christmas gift box. Early that evening, a boy had shown up before her and, without any explanation, placed the gift box on the table in the hallway and then strode away, avoiding being hit by the ripples of anger the delivery would surely cause.

Just before disappearing, the boy shouted, 'Chila, Dionisio sent that. He sends greetings to you, to Mr. Terefo, and especially to Zunilda.'

Mama Chila walked to the box. She opened

it with disdain. The mere fact that it came from that man was reason enough to be the object of contempt. Anyway, she opened it. Its content was what she had assumed, being the Christmas holydays and all. It was customary in these places for suitors to send wine or liquor, nuts and fruits to the parents of the girls they fancied. This action under different circumstances would have been seen as pleasant, but Dionisio did not appear to them like the best of prospects, and Zunilda was still just a girl. At least that's how she saw her, and it would be even worse with her grandfather—when he found out, he would surely feel great displeasure.

She finished opening the box. What happened next can only be described by comparing it to one of Picasso or Dalí's paintings. Her hands multiplied. The bottles, nuts and fruits rose in awkward flight reaching such heights that for brief moments they were lost from human eyes, just to reappear, quickly, in their path toward the destruction of all their forms.

Zunilda did not ask anything about it. As usual, she went to her room, said the prayers of that day, blew out the candle and gave life to the bed with her presence. She closed her eyes and dreamed of Dionisio. Yes, for the very first time she dreamed of something other than God and his kingdom of angels and saints. And what a strange dream it was. This man, Dionisio, spoke to her and his voice slithered through the cracks of the window. He told her that he was there, waiting, 'if you hear me, light the candle back on.' He spoke about love and about things she still did not understand.

She woke up startled. Thinking that perhaps it had not been a dream, she approached the window. A breath of fresh breeze came through the slots between the woods, and she felt as if someone had given her a gentle kiss. Then she strained to see something out there, but the darkness of the night denied her any possibility. She went back to bed, prayed some more and returned to her world of purity.

Her following days and nights passed with restless dreams. Zunilda no longer hunted butterflies. A kind of fear had taken a hold of her: she had turned each of her actions into a consequence of Dionisio's actions. She would go nowhere by herself. Now Leonides accompanied her everywhere at all times. From the moment she'd taken possession of this assignment, there was no way to avoid her. Every attempt by Dionisio to provoke an encounter with the one he had decided would be his woman was in vain. Not because he gave up, no, but because she had succumbed to that pre-existing fear—which grew despite the inseparable presence of her guardian. Dionisio did not have any other alternative but to face all those who in one way or the other denied him what he already considered his.

Everyone knew the famous saying: "He who drinks *Brugal* either fights or gets things done." He had decided to drink the famous rum;

not to fight, but to 'get thigs done'—and this he meant in the literal sense of the words. He uncapped the bottle, poured the first potential mouthful of the liquid on the ground —because that was the poison sip, "for the dead", they say— and then drank in gulps, as if to welcome the urgent arrival of his courage.

In the region, everyone knew about Zunilda's grandfather's character. He was a respectable man, whose word was not to be taken lightly, and who demanded the same from any man who offered him his. Dionisio was afraid. The fear of not fearing. He knew that once the doors were opened to see the young woman, instantly other doors would be closed for him: in his world of freedom. On the other hand, he wanted Zunilda; felt a need for her, and this was a force greater than fear. He had started the journey. He would not turn back.

The night had grown darker. The moon had hidden and nobody knew where—and this made the stars hang brighter up there. Dionisio looked at them. Only in them could he find something close to the beauty of the feeling that now dressed his soul. He had greeted the old man, paid his respects. In exchange, he had been granted permission to go see Zunilda every Wednesday.

'From seven to eight, on Wednesdays. From seven to eight, you can come and say hello,' he had been told. And it had seemed enough for him.

One, two, three… many Wednesdays passed, but his quest did not prosper. Every time he tried to establish contact with Zunilda, something arose that prevented it. There was always the grandmother, Leonides, or some other person—like a wall of interference. Verbal communication between him and the girl was never possible. There were only looks and half smiles. He wanted more. He was starving for her voice. He wanted to devour her words and plant words of his own in her ears.

A few other Wednesdays came and went by and everything remained the same. The living room did not relent on its new-found power of attraction. It had become the favorite meeting spot in the house. Since the arrival of Dionisio, it had displaced the arbor as the place to concentrate an audience; so much so that, at times, he believed himself part of the casting in a theater play. One of those improvised in the backyards of churches to celebrate the days of patron saints and their festivities.

Zunilda was growing more beautiful each day, and Dionisio's nights more intense.

'If you're awake, light the candle. Come closer to the wall and tell me you love me; I want to hear it from your voice.' She heard this. Once again, she thought she was dreaming.

He repeated the message. This time neither

the old woman nor Leonides were there, only her
fear was. When she realized that it was all real, that
he was there, she felt the scare of her life.

'It's Okay. I know you're there listening;
you'll talk to me soon enough. I'll come every Wednesday after greeting your folks; and I know that,
when you discover your wings, then we will fly together.'

He returned many other Wednesdays. The
living room was waiting for him as always, dressed
in a time span filled with grins and half glances.
There was an immense thirst for words. Everything
was silent until the farewell. Everyone ought to wait
until the following Wednesday for the next meeting.
Everyone except him and her.

'If you're listening, light up the candle.
Don't make me wait any longer; tell me something.
Don't you see I can't live without you anymore?'

She resisted. She didn't want to light the
candle. If she did, he would notice that she was
awake, that she had been listening to him every
Wednesday, and his words had grown in her ears
like poppies in the field. Then he would ask for more than words, and she was not sure she could com-
ply with the possible requests nor resist the tempta-
tion.

He came back another night. She didn't light the candle. She would never do it. He always asked, but no, she wouldn't. Something in her would prevent it forever.

What she did was open the window. She let the stars shine on her with their light.

She liked starlight and its infinite variations in intensity. She liked the cool breeze, and now she liked Dionisio, too. All the elements were there, coming together to make the smile of touch possible. That's how it was supposed to be. She could have opened the window a minute earlier, while he was still there, but she did not. Only when she was sure that Dionisio and his words were already part of the world of absences, only then she showed her head and let the heavens dress it with their beauty as an ornament.

'I think and think about you; I tell you this a thousand times. I spend every night thinking about your love. I want to know if you love me, too. I think and I think of you; I can't rip you out of my mind.'

The voice had a melody to it. As if it danced with the notes that flowed from the guitar. First, it went through the cracks in the wood, and then continued its way inside… to her heart. The man was there, accompanied by others, making public his despair. She felt that she was in debt and opened the window.

'Thank you,' she said, and then disappeared, but not before planting in him that moment of happiness that would feed his ego until their next meeting.

Dionisio was patient. After many Wednesdays, Zunilda got used to him, to his voice, his words, and his promises of eternal happiness—what she believed to be lies and the parts she believed could be true. She became so accustomed to him, to his presence, that now fear was a displaced concept. In its place, little by little, sensations and brave emotions had taken shelter. The same ones that made her think about him—and desire him. She had discovered her wings and wanted to fly.

Everything was silent. Only the sound of the crickets sweetened the minutes. The stars looked more distant than ever. Judging by the prevailing stillness, this should not be a special night. Dionisio crossed the border between hour nine and hour ten. Then he went through the seconds of this last hour until he reached the window. He got closer. He was already saying the words:

'Here I am, as always, my Zuni,' but it was not necessary. To his amazement, she opened the window without him asking.

'Take me with you,' she said. He could not give credit to her words. For a few seconds, he was totally silent.

'Take me with you,' she repeated as she climbed onto the window frame. He took her into his arms. Together they took flight. They drank from the honey of the moon that night, and populated it with the negation of the singular.

The next morning rose dressed in discontent. They could not accept that Zunilda, that girl who had been raised with diligence to be an example to follow, the one everyone had chosen to represent the virgin, had been capable of such an act.

For days, nothing was heard from the couple. Everyone inquired. It was rumored that they were at Luis Manuel and Lourdes's house: and more than one took a walk around—for, perhaps, they might run into the missing lovers.

Chapter Four

Leonides's time

Zunilda's departure provoked an immense void around the worlds that she used to frequent. Some sort of black hole: the monster that all galaxies have, which slowly drags every energy-carrying body towards its center. In it, the grandmother's anger was offed, as well as the grandfather's jealousy, and the curiosity of all those who day after day fed their fantasies with the uncertainty of whether or not they would be able to witness a kiss, a look or at least a word from him that invisibly dared to cross the distance from his lips to her ears, to ask for another word that might want to accompany it on its journey through the paths that lead to plural forms.

All energy appeared to have been exhausted

by the event of the rupture of time. There, right where she allowed the concept of "girl" to die in order to transition to the concept of "woman." It seemed that everything happened in the same manner. It did not. As it is known, in all consumption of energy, there is also the creation and release of other energies that, in a way, come to alter the relative stillness that prevails in the brief time after the initial action. This is how we can explain the reasons behind the moment of Leonides.

What she felt when she found out about Zunilda's escape, we cannot define it either as sadness or joy. This is so because it was a mix of emotions that invaded her world.

At the beginning, she was enraged. She had the same reasons as the others to believe that what had happened in fact was an infamy, a total inconsideration. She had lived to protect her, to become almost her shadow, to avoid this outcome; but naive as she was, she was tempted —and succumbed.

After the fury, sadness took over. A sadness that covered all the corners of her being, and could reach even farther. She felt sad to be alone. Sad not to have someone to make her happy or even unhappy. It didn't matter anymore. She did not know how this feeling had risen, but ever since the ungrateful Zunilda left, she felt lonelier than ever —and the strength of desire had made it more intense.

Sad, angry, and even happy. At times, yes,

she felt happy. Deep within herself, and despite the other emotions, there, in some corner of her being, Leonides' zealously guarded a little place for the feelings of joy that from time to time peeked out of the sadness. Yes, despite it all, she felt joy for Zunilda, for her Dionisio Mercado, and for everything that was probably happening to her by his side.

She thought all of that could be happening to herself. If only they had not had that book with them. If only Luis had hidden it before the military came that day, if only... Everything would have been different. She would have had the opportunity to be tempted… to succumb in the same way.

Not Luis, though, her first love. Luis was not meant for her. Things happened the way they happened and now nothing could be different.

She remembered that afternoon and the following days like a cracking of sorts. As if suddenly the pathways of life had been twisted. They disappeared him, and now she was here, remembering him, living in vicarious longing this passion through the romance between Zunilda and her Dionisio. Remembering him, she had become a place where diverse emotions converged. She didn't want to eat; she did not speak —sometimes she laughed, sometimes she cried. She was the new spotlight. Everyone looked at her now while Zunilda had slowly entered oblivion.

*****

"Hey, mister, you have not said a word in a while." Fernando said.

"Yeah, Fernando, that's right. I was in my memory again. I was just going through the lives of Zunilda, Dionisio, and Leonides. Revisiting how things took place."

"Cousin Leonides… that seems interesting to me. They locked her up. And what happened to Luis. Damn, straight from a fiction novel!"

"Novelesque, yes, but as real as being Dominicans or coming from times that still carry their own labels: Trujillo and Balaguer, for example, not to mention others. But I was saying how, maybe, things really happened to them. Most likely, they were in the process of sharing a kiss when they saw the soldiers arrive. Maybe they separated a little to save face and, in their haste, Luis forgot to hide the book."

*****

'But what do we have here? A communist book! This is interesting.' One of the Militia men said.

'I found it.'

'Really? You just… found it? Be a man and tell the truth.' The soldier pressed. 'Let's see, you, young lady, do you know Valerio?'

'No.'

'Another one who won't say a word, uh! Take them away!'

And away they took them. For many hours no one heard a word about their whereabouts. That was until Mapenga arrived.

'But, Chila, what did that girl do?' Mapenga asked.
'What girl?'
'Leonides! Don't you know? They took her. She was thrown in jail along with that boy: Luis.'
'What are you saying?'
'The truth! Better let Terefo know; and be quick! The way things are right now, no one ever knows. These people take you in alive and bring you out dead.'
'May God save us.'

They told Grandpa all about it, and the old man brought her back. But not before she got slapped a couple of times by the soldiers as they questioned her about Valerio and her relationship with him.

'It's over! You can't leave the house, much less with that Luis fellow,' said the grandmother. She helped her to bed and then left.

How is Luis doing? She thought, and then wandered around in her pain.

*****

The world was square. Infinitely square. That is how Luis perceived it. He could not see a thing. The all-encompassing darkness prevented it. Had that not been the case, any other possibility of seeing would have also been null. They had hit him in the face—his eyes were swollen shut.

'How did you meet Valerio? Where is Valerio? Who are Valerio's accomplices? Answer, damn it!'

'I don't know. I don't know what you're talking about! I don't know any Valerio!' He cried. Then he asked, 'Leonides? Where is Leonides? What did you do to her?'

'She is not here. If you were to tell me where Valerio is, then we could talk about her.'

'I do not know. I do not know. I do not know any Valerio.'

'This one won't let up. Take him to The Night.'

The Night was a narrow and humid cell. Once there, after having traveled a distance similar to that of a goodbye, Luis felt exiled. He had been deprived of everything. He thought that the same thing would be happening to Leonides—if they had not killed her yet.

He realized how absurd the moment was. Exhausted, he surrendered to sleep—unsure if he would ever wake up.

*****

Luis's absence grew to such a degree that there was no corner in Leonides' world that did not miss him. The poppies lost their redness, and although they were now dressed in green, she couldn't seize the sense of hope the color green was supposed to represent.

The leaves on the ground and the sound they made when her feet crushed them annoyed her. It was a statement of the acceleration of the decomposition process of the forms. Yet the words were silent. They managed to travel the distance from her lips to her ears but failed to convey the message that should have been there. Her life was moving at zero speed. She had entered the eye of the storm; and although everything around her was shaking aggressively, she felt inert—not at peace, just inert.

She glanced at the Mirabal sisters' portrait. She didn't know why, but for some time now her soul had been hung on the wall, next to the image of those three women. She no longer cared about the concept of trilogies. She had always known that everything came in bunches of three: God, Homeland and Freedom; Duarte, Sánchez and Mella; Patria, Minerva and María Teresa.

She did not care. Besides, they were four now, were they not? She liked to hang on to the feeling that emanated from that portrait. In it she could read immense tenderness in María Teresa's eyes and braids, in Patria's elegance (which went beyond the limits imposed by the portrait frame), and in Minerva's courage. She had always known about Minerva. She liked to listen to the stories told about her.

'That girl had courage! What with leaving the boss standing in the middle of the dance floor! She just walked away and left him there like you leave remains of food on a dirty plate.'

'Well, she sure did. Few people could have done something like that.'

'Now, one can only wonder what happened *before* she did that.'

'They say Trujillo made a pass at her even though he knew she was married.'

'You believe that? Seems to me he provoked her. He wanted to have an excuse to get rid of her.'

'Maybe so. After that, it didn't take long for them to turn up dead—them and those who were supposedly conspiring against the regime.'

She liked hearing about Minerva, and even more now. She felt that somehow life had taken them down the same path. Manolo had been taken away from Minerva, and so had Luis—he could be dead already.

The pain grew bigger in her chest. She took her eyes off the portrait. Like a robot, she went to the trunk. She knew they were inside—like vampires afraid of the light, hiding in there. She had seen them before. Grandma had them in case things got difficult. She opened the chest.

'We need to keep these portraits within reach. In case the authorities come by and ask to see them,' Grandma always said.

With unusual courage, she drove her hand all the way in. She felt the cold flat glass. First Trujillo[5] came out; then, Balaguer[6].

When she had them before her eyes, she felt like she was drowning between two beasts. She threw them to the ground, and instinctively stomped on them. The floor turned red. From the portraits, she saw them emerge to bite her feet; and she ran. She ran until she found an exit way

---

[5] *Rafael Leonidas Trujillo*, Dominican dictator from 1930 to 1961—he was assassinated by a group of patriots.
[6] *Joaquín Balaguer*, Dominican dictator from 1962 to 1996.

toward madness.

Chapter Five

Pirán

When she woke up, the two monsters were gone. What's more, they were not in her memory the way they should have been. On top of white pedestals, the lights of candles fought each other over the darkness. Time had become light. Everything had become light.

Leonides looked all over the parts of the world in which she was now walking and concluded that she was dead. So much luminous splendor could only be possible within the perimeters of heaven. Let alone the aroma of penetrating essences enervating her senses. And there was this extended sense of peace. All the saints were there, and she perched on their altars to see them better. She flew from one kingdom to the next on the wings of ecstasy. She was naked, completely naked; and when she realized it, she wanted to cover herself.

'Don't be afraid, my girl,' said an old woman who, now at a visible spot, reminded her of the priestesses of Greek temples in the pages of heavy encyclopedias.

The lady was dressed in white. She stepped closer and took her hand—as she did so, Leonides felt that her world was surrendering to the power of that woman's tenderness. She allowed to be led. The woman made her enter the small pool that contained the aromatic bath. Mint leaves and other herbs covered her body.

'You are with Pirán, and the strength of God keeps you company.'

'Am I dead?'

'No, you live. And from now on, you will be more alive than ever. Drink, let the water flood your deserts. First, we must feed your body, and then we will mend your soul.'

Leonides drank and fell into a deep sleep.

Chapter Six

Fernando

"Are you Okay, Fernando?"

"No, I feel like I'm leaving. From time to time, I feel like I'm leaving from myself. Something here inside my head pressures me and takes away my consciousness. Leaves me blank, weak. Sometimes I don't hear a thing. It must be the tumor. It has already grown too much."

"Probably… like the last time. The relatively good thing about all this is that the doctors already know your case well. This time, when they operate on you, they just have to follow the same path they opened before." I joked. He laughed again.

"Yes, I hope. I'm also worried about therapy after the operation, you know."

"Sure, but don't think too much about it.

The important thing now is that you come out of the surgery well. Remember, you have to take it easy. Rest, so that your cells are in order when doctors operate."

"Easy for you to say, but being in my place, well… not easy."

"I know. In any case, therapy is something you should not postpone. If you had done it the first time, when they removed part of that tumor, most likely its growth would have stopped; and now this second procedure, perhaps it would not have been necessary."

"Sure, yeah, whatever. This is bullshit, though. Let me tell you, all this moving about and driving here and there, all this hustle, sometimes I feel like dropping it all, all lost, and ending things once and for all. This suffering. If it weren't for Dylan, I swear I would do it."

"Well, it's good that you have Dylan then. Now, if your bond with him is not strong enough for you, remember that your brothers will always have other anchors to keep you floored in this world when the gales want to drag your boat towards the distance."

"Damn, that sounds good!"

"See, I like it that way. Move away from sadness and enjoy the beauty that can be found at any given moment, in any play on words," I said this to bring him farther from those thoughts that lurked like a starved wolf.

Two years had gone by since his first diagnosis.

'It's a tumor. It covers almost the entire right side of the occipital cavity. It must be removed as quickly as possible, because it is constantly growing. It will eventually obstruct everything around it.'

The doctor had spoken calmly, and as naturally as anyone in a common dialogue.

'We lack the technology to intervene here. We could not guarantee the successful and complete functioning of the sensory faculties and motor skills of this young man after the procedure. Can you try to take him to the United States? They do have the necessary equipment for this type of surgery.'
'Yes, doctor, we'll try. God willing, we can get him a visa,' I said.
'God willing,' said Fernando.

*****

The day went by like in a movie. Above, a radiant sun appeared to have paused midway on its way to the higher sky, and a fresh breeze was blowing—as a contradiction. There was optimism in everyone who, like us, was waiting in line. Somehow, we had convinced ourselves God would help us to overcome all obstacles.

I thought about the American consul. It was time to say my "prayer": a series of words that, all together, formed a sort of my spiritual protection against everything that could be averse to me.

'I offer myself to the three divine persons: Father, Son and Holy Spirit. May God himself speak for me, softening hard hearts. Crucified son, son of the Virgin Mary, keep me tonight, and tomorrow during the day. May my blood not be seen nor my eyes be corrupted. May the eyes of my enemies be blindfolded for me. Once again, I offer myself to the three divine persons: Father, Son, and Holy Spirit.'

I repeated the prayer the entire way, from the entrance until the moment that we reached the small consul booth.

'Shit! It's the Chinese. We got the Chinese!' I said in a low voice. They had warned us: 'If you go to the Chinese, forget everything. No one can convince him. He will not give you a visa.'

'Your documents, please.'

'Here they are.' I said, then I handed him the papers and the X-rays, which clearly showed the fatal tumor on Fernando's head.

'And you want to go to do the surgery in the United States?'

'Yes, sir.'

'And where will you be staying there?'

'We have relatives there.'

'And who is going to cover all the expenses?'

'We will,' I said—after thinking for several seconds.

'All his papers are in order, but at the moment we don't have a visa available for you.' He said as he returned the papers to us.

*****

'Doctor, they denied us the visa.'

'Then you must take the risks and operate here. If you don't, he could die in less than a year. Do you understand? It is a matter of life or death.'

'Yes, doctor, we understand. It is just not easy to imagine him mute, or blind, or worse… he could die in there, too.'

'I'm telling you, it's a risk that must be taken. Anyway, it's up to you.'

'Doctor, do you think it could be resolved in Italy?'

'It's possible. I heard they have the equipment in Milan.'

'Well, then it will be a matter of seeing

things clearly, because Fernando just came from Italy; he lives and works over there.'

'Then, of course. Expedite your efforts. If that does not work either, then… remember, we must proceed as soon as possible.' The doctor concluded.

*****

"Hey, Fernando, tell me what those days were like, before and after the first operation? I was not around then."

"Well, what would they be like? Imagine! I was very scared. It's no easy thing to hear that you are dying; that they will open your head and you may never wake up again. All I could do was pray. I entrusted myself to the *Virgen de la Altagracia*. 'I put my spirit in your hands,' I told her, and the peace that came over me felt as if my prayers had pleased her, and in return she made me feel at peace and confident. I had already experienced something like this, surely you remember, when we were children. I was about seven years old when they took me to Higüey. We went to see the virgin because of the bone that was sticking out of my back. Remember? Well, right then and there I began to have faith in her...

'Virgin Mary, I promise you, if you heal my child, I will take him to your house so you can see him and he can thank you for your help, and I will share twenty pesos among the beggars in the square. I promise you, dear Virgin.'

"That's what I remember Mom said as we prayed before the Virgin's image, the image of Saint Joseph, and that of the Child Jesus. Because the painting people venerate as that of the *Virgen de la Altagracia* is truly the representation of the Holy Family. So, you have Joseph, representing the father; Mary, representing the mother; and Jesus, who is the son."

"Yes, it's a very beautiful concept expressed by the artist in that work; but, well, we were talking about the trip and how finally the deadlines were met."

"January twenty-first, 1974, arrived early. There are days that, due to their great emotional load, you start living them in advance, as if they were granted permission to use the time of the days that precede them. That's what happened to us then. All our vital functions were influenced and moved at the speed of the intensity of our passion for the trip. The tickets were already paid for. I remember that a few days before we had been to Payiyo's house, the driver and owner of the excursion bus. There we made the payment that guaranteed the seats in *La Cuca*. That's what they called the colorful bus, whose capacity did not exceed thirty-six people. Payiyo, of course, took more than sixty—all in his eagerness to help others. 'It's just that everyone wants to go, and I feel sorry to leave them behind,' he said." Fernando smiled with perhaps a bit of melancholy.

"At the bottom, La Cuca was painted a light blue, or sky blue, as people called it. Above, it had tinted glass windows that protected from the sun. It was a beautiful bus, that's the truth. I remember approaching it and touching it, as if it were a circus attraction, something you didn't see every day. Then I felt a mix of joy and envy at the same time. Yes, I remember it clearly. 'I wish I were going to Higüey,' I said to myself while, at the same time, realizing the impossibility of that desire," I commented.

"Then we heard Payiyo's convincing voice: 'Come here, kids, aren't you Lidia's children? Come, the seats are running out!' And we went to him. He looked at us tenderly. I don't know why, but I always saw that same look in people's eyes towards us. As if seeing us made them feel that protective instinct for free. 'Lidia's kids and the late Isa's, now that was a man, dammit!' I had heard more than once, and somehow my ego was fed by the possession of a father I hardly remembered. 'Which one is going to Higüey?' Payiyo asked. And you said it was you. I remember it perfectly. The joy was so evident throughout your body, as if it couldn't stay inside," Fernando said.

"You know, Fernando, I think I lived that trip with the same intensity as you did."

"Yes, it was something we all talked about for many days, which we all enjoyed directly or indirectly. I stayed awake. I couldn't sleep that night. Something prevented it. I closed my eyes and, one after the other, potential inconveniences swarmed into my mind like flies. I told myself, 'If I fall asleep, we'll be late in the morning, maybe Mom won't wake up; then we would miss the bus, because there's no way they would wait for us.' No, that night wasn't for sleeping. I stayed awake—as the saying goes: Not wanting to, but wanting."

Fernando kept recounting the events with delirium, almost with hope. As if he wanted to paint for me all the landscapes and details I was not able see, so I wouldn't feel sad about missing the trip.

"There were still some stars in the sky that early morning. 'Walk faster,' our mother said, 'walk, or they'll leave us behind,' and we quickened our pace. It didn't matter that the thorns of the mesh hurt our feet. We did not mind. We continued to battle with the mud on the road. 'Once we reach the capital borderlines, just a little farther, you will see the sea,' she said. 'It looks like it's a big, sweet potato crop. Something like when the wind gently moves the peanut leaves, the waters sway, and one feels like dancing with them,' I heard her say. The excitement of the journey and the desire to know the sea became bigger. 'Yes, take me; I want to see the sea and the Basílica. They say it's very big; almost touches the sky,' I told her, and she could feel, almost breathe, my passion. 'Yes, honey, it is very big. It is the house of God and our Mother's. You are going to thank her for having fixed that bone. Remember, that's the most important part. We are going to pay off that promise.' 'Yes, I know,' I answered.

And we got to the road, washed our feet and put on our shoes. My heart was dancing. I was jumping with excitement (she could feel it), as if I wanted to accompany the musicians who had settled in the back of the bus, and, out of tune, sang *Por ahí María se va.* On the way, we saw the caves of the Three Eyes, the sea and the Cathedral, imposing —from afar, we saw its arches."

"Oh yes, the Cathedral. Tell me about that. From what you told me back then, it was something that really impacted you," I interrupted.

"Those arches were huge. The top one almost reaching into the clouds, like a staircase leading to who-knows-where in the heights. We got closer, and the square was full of beggars. With every step we took, a voice would rise, attempting to be heard: 'Friend, over here, here; give me something. It was the Virgin who brought you; madam, come here.'

The voices followed us as we moved, and that's how the entire walk went, from the entrance of the square until we reached the Cathedral's door. It was shaped like a big M, decorated with small figures that seemed to emerge from the mahogany wood it was made of. It was an immense door. And later, when we entered, it was as if we were stepping into a magical place. Everywhere we looked, there were large windows, and from them, reflected by the sunlight, the saints and angels seemed to be flying. It was something like when we lived out in the countryside, and little bits of sun would come through the cracks in the palm wood planks. Some appeared to be round and others had different shapes, and I saw them slowly move around the room."

"'Yes, of course. It was one of the many ways we connected with the Cosmos," I agreed.

"And the Virgin, man, we could barely see her, because of all the jewelry hanging in the frame that enclosed her. These were the offerings. So much gold! So much shine! And the people outside, in the blazing heat, starving, but full of faith. That, I can say for sure, the people who go there, they overflow with faith and gratitude.

After seeing the Virgin and paying off our promise, we bought sweets and some little medals as souvenirs to make those days memorable. And then it was time to return. The musicians, tired, had placed the guitar and the drum on the ground. The driver finally rested from the mockery of the chorus, improvised by the younger ones. They were no longer repeating that nasty mantra: 'the driver has a small one, the driver has a small one... the driver has a small one.'

We were dozing off when the cow crossed the highway. We felt the crash and staggered in the same direction and rhythm as the bus, which finally took us with it to kiss the ground. A few minutes later, one by one, we crawled out to safety, and then some helped those who couldn't do it on their own.

'Doña Lidia!' someone was shouting as if trying to wake her up. And then I saw my mother lying on the floor, her eyes closed, with a paleness that looked like a shortcut that brought all times together. In her face, instead of her features, I saw my Dad's face again. Motionless, without any color; and then I imagined the coffin, and felt the cold of endless distance. Then, involuntarily, I screamed! I remember myself screaming, 'Holy Virgin, help me!' And then I saw her open her eyes! She moved her arm toward me and smiled. I felt a gap opening, a path through which it was still possible to escape from orphanhood. Since then, I have faith. I thank the Virgin the same way I thank Leonides for being there, supporting me always."

"What Leonides? Cousin Leonides? The nun?"

"Yes, that one. Only now she is no longer a nun."

"Yes, I heard. What we do not understood is how she went from one thing to the other."

"The truth is that it must have been hard for her to change her lifestyle. She told me once, after she went with the Carmelite nuns to Spain and spent time in that convent, she had realized her true vocation was not to serve God in that way. She grew weary of being alone; said she liked to read, and reading helped her during those days of cloister. Sometimes she got lost in the stories she read, but managed to come back to reality somehow. She also said she enjoys looking back and recognizing herself as one of the characters in those books."

"She was addicted to reading!"

"Yes, we could say that. As I was saying, she used to go into the stories so much that, for her, sometimes their fiction was more real than reality itself. This one time, while reading *Azul*, she was with Bertha, one of the characters of *El Castillo del sol*. She didn't know how, but there she was: in the ballroom, under the lights of beautiful chandeliers. She wasn't a young woman blessed with the arrival of spring on her being, but one of them she was anyway: sad, dark-eyed and filled with all the emotions of those other girls she was emulating. And then, she saw Bertha and the other girls running away—each with their own prince.

In the end, as always, she ruminated on how difficult it would be for her to be happy. I was sort of shocked when I heard her say she would leave her habits for good. The truth is that she had already hung the habits off. From that one day when her eyes met those of the owner of the winery she had entered by chance."

*****

'How can we help you, angel?'

'You can call me 'Sister'. I am no angel, sir. Sister Leonides.'

'Sure, as you wish. But the truth is that you illuminated this place with your presence… like an angel.'

'Come on, come on, more respect.'

'Oh, but if I mean no disrespect. I'm just saying that you look like God Himself put a little extra dedication on your beauty, that's all. Also, well, I am here at your service. And, I say, in case one day you feel the need to throw away all those rags you're wearing and which must weigh a ton, I am here to give you a hand. My name is Nemencio, by the way; and I believe that you and me, we were born to be together.'

'May God forgive you!' She said, in shock, and strode out quickly, as if to prevent getting reached by the man's sins.

She should not have returned, yet she went back many times. She wanted to prove to herself that she was strong; that she would not succumb to the temptations of worldly life. She thought she would make it. It never crossed her mind that she could be wrong. Not too long after, she discovered that, for her, the divine plan was summed up in loving and allowing herself to be loved... and so it was.

One afternoon she left the convent and, when she returned, it was only to offer her farewells and say thank you. Outside, offering her a new life, was Nemencio.

*****

"And how come they live in Italy now?"

"I don't know. I never asked her. We are all together there now."

"It's a small world, isn't it!"

"That's right. What I'm saying, I guess, is that she has been like a sister to me. Always there for me, before and after the operation. And then you and Carolina came. Those days with you were very good."

"Yes, they were. I never thought we would travel to Paris together."

"Neither did I. To think that we as children were herding cows back in the countryside! Who would have thought?!"

"Yeah, true. Sometimes the things we think farthest from us are well within reach. Some troubadour said that in a song."

"Yeah! It is just a matter of choice. We turned something that seemed to ruin our day into a positive experience. I remember being a little sad because you were leaving for Spain. I confess I got happy when the inspector informed that you would not be able to travel just then. Your Passport had expired and you needed to get some sort of waiver. It would take you a few days. I thought it was great to be able to hang out together for just a little longer. Then we had to worry about finding accommodations, and combed the city looking for a hotel with at least one available room; but since Fashion Week was upon us, everything was busy in Milan. 'So, what do we do now?' I asked somewhat upset. 'Where I live, there is not enough room for another soul.' 'Paris… Let's go to Paris,' you replied, and so we did.

Now all that is past. I feel as if just now we went back in time to that moment—when everything was a *maybe*. The time prior to the unfulfilled desire of visiting *Moulin Rouge*, before the city lights and its museums, and the fascinating ride on that train that fills the Alps in its eagerness to get to León." Fernando said. His heart undecided on being heavy or light.

"You know, Fernando, I'm also glad this is how it happened. Those were very happy days." I said, and my eyes fell again on the coming and going of those tiny birds that circled high above, between the white of the clouds and the faint blue of the waters. Again, I became an object of abstraction.

Chapter Seven

Luis

'You are with Pirán, and the strength of God accompanies you,' the old woman repeated in one of her many sessions. And Leonides felt the positive aura that came from her.

'I am with Pirán. May the strength of God be with me,' Leonides said, as if to give in to the power of the moment she was experiencing.

'Your God is only as great as your faith in him.'

'My God is as great as I want him to be.'

'And tell me, Leonides, how much do you believe in God?"

'Very much. I believe very much.'

'Then ask him with faith, with great faith, to bring Luis back to you.'

'No, that cannot be… because Luis is dead.

You know this.'

'I know? That's not true. I know nothing. I'm nothing more than an old woman that has lived a lot and has learned to walk the paths of life. Come on, ask him!'

'I don't know, Mrs. Pirán; I don't think I should.'

'*I* am telling you that you should. Remember, God is the size of your faith.'

Only three months after her arrival in this place, what would be her wild card on the tortuous road back to normality, Leonides already showed signs of surprising improvement. She was much more connected to reality; and whenever the image of Luis happened to enter her present, she jumped into some memory that would provide her with at least a hint of happiness.

'It's time,' said Pirán. 'I think you're ready for the truth.'

'What truth?' Leonides asked.

'Your truth. We are all waiting for a moment of truth that we must face. In your case, I think it's time for you to learn the truth about Luis.'

'About Luis? You have news about Luis?'

'He is alive.'

Leonides looked at her for a long minute. Both in silence.

'Don't play with me, Mrs. Pirán.'

'No, he is alive. I tell you this not so that you suffer, but so that you start getting used to the idea that you will soon be together.'

'Where is he? I want to see him!'

'You'll see him, but now it's time to rest; you must rest over this anguish to be able to resist what seeing him again will cause you. Here, drink some tea, and sleep.'

She drank again the liquid that was like a shortcut—a sort of rapid tunnel to the place of her subconscious: where she believed she could achieve total relaxation.

'What have they done to you?' She exclaimed, seeing him with two crutches that, more than help, seemed to prevent his painful attempts to reach her. He did not say anything. He remained in the distance of that dream.

She woke up scared. Now she had an almost certain idea of what their encounter would be like. Something like a foretaste of the time to come. She had seen him without his right leg, and thought, if all of that were true, she would still love him the same.

*****

The sun covered the morning spaces with its tender clarity. Leonides left the bed, and, after drinking a cup of coffee (submerging herself in its aroma), headed out to the sanctuary.

'I am with Pirán, and may the strength of God be with me.'

'So be it, girl, so be it. Light your candle and come help me. The person I'm dealing with today needs us; he needs us deeply,' said Pirán.

Leonides was surprised. She could not recall a single time when the old woman had asked for help to heal someone. Besides, she did not know the first thing about healing—or did not think she did. When she approached the patient, she noticed that his head was partially covered. She did not know the reason, but deduced that the bandages and all those overlapping leaves were part of some treatment to heal his wounds.

'Come, come closer; let God manifest himself through you.'

'Madam, you know that I don't know how to proceed.'

'Come closer, it is not you. God will act *through* you. Remember that we are only instruments in His divine plan. Come, help me, we must get to that remote place where he takes refuge. He went too far away in his attempt to escape from the cruel reality he had to live through; but not so far that we can't bring him back.'

She made a pause. Her gaze rose. She then looked back at them and carried on.

'Little by little, we will populate his mind with pieces of memories—pleasant memories that push away those that, like woodworm, ravaged the happiness off his existence. Yes, yes, we are going to bring him to the present, to our present.

Come, give me your hand, let us make a chain of positive vibrations.'

They held each other's hands with great strength. The old woman said:

'At this moment, I give you Luis. You are going to cure him. He is somewhat battered, but you are going to cure him. In time, all his wounds will heal. Those inside and outside, they will heal. I'm telling you; I know my stuff! Have faith. He will heal.'

Then she remained silent. As if by doing so, she meant to lessen Leonide's shock. As if she were handing Leonides all of her strength. Luis was in the fetal position, reflecting the degree of his emotional setback. So much distance in his mind had been travelled backward that there was no longer any room left for him to become more absent. Then he started to subtract from himself. That's why he was like this: his knees grazing his belly, his hands touching his knees: a lousy sketch of a circle. He had shrunk into something like a response to the call of his mother's navel: he visualized it as a tunnel whose roundness one could crawl through into another dimension. One whose distance was indisputably infinite.

She looked at him with sad eyes. For several seconds she remained there, remembering everything that had happened, and almost letting herself be carried away by that feeling which was almost a preamble to the acceptance of defeat. Then she took a couple of steps closer, placed both hands on Luis's head, and caressed him with the same tenderness she as a girl used to caress the pigeons in mama Chila's bower. Luis shrank even more. He adjusted himself in such a way that in his posture one could read the satiation of the thirst of longing.

Chapter Eight

Farewell

Life is a repetitive act. That's why we don't get tired of living or dying. For every moment we live, we die another moment; and, so, we go from life to death and from death to life until we reach the time of ultimate uncertainty and absence.

'Chila passed,' someone said. I remember this perfectly. 'She died,' he emphasized. Then I saw in my mother's eyes everything that was left to say, plus the emptiness that Mama Chila's absence already caused.

The man was right, she had died. Her soul had returned to pick up the body it had left behind. I guess she didn't want to leave any evidence of her time in our company. Pale, almost imperceptible, what remained of her presence spoke to us of her irrevocable departure. Although, to tell the truth, she had left a long time before. At the very moment in which Father Miguel finished offering the last rites to Grandpa Terefo. We saw her then enter a trance. She contorted and spoke in tongues.

We all thought she had had a nervous breakdown, but, as the days passed, we realized that what we had witnessed were the early signs of her death. Mama Chila had died that day, too. Instead of one, there were two corpses we would have to deal with. What we didn't know was that one of them would stay with us, and would spend some more time searching for her soul.

"Do you think it would be fine to tell the story of the grandparents?" I asked.

"I'm fine with it. What about me? Have you already thought about what the end of my story will be like?"

"No, Fernando; and I think I will never have it; at least the way you suggest."

"Why not? Everyone knows I'm going to die."

"Yes, that's right. We also know that we are all going to die. What we don't know is who will get to see who die first. That's why I couldn't possibly have a real ending to your memories. You should know that while we are present, we die and are re-born at every moment. If I am present when you are past, then I will know your end. Otherwise, you must be the one to write about me. I like to write from memory."

"Remembering is good; it is like being in a spot where you can watch the movie you have been filming, directing and acting since the day you were born."

"Yes, Fernando, memory is the shortest distance between two times."

"True; through memory, we get a little closer to all those things of ours that we left behind."

"Memory is the key that opens our doors to the past and allows us entry to the very center— where, somehow, it is still the present."

"Well said. It allows us to venture into the journey of other times."

"I agree with you. Other thoughts are not as clear as the notion of memory. Yet, we know they can inform us about things to come. Although, of course, it is all the opposite from memory, it is still quite similar."

"You are making things very complicated for me right now. In this case, what I mean is that we are here now, bur tomorrow we will be some-where else. Now we are together, enjoying ourselves in this place, but, in a few hours, I will be in Italy. Then everything will have changed."

"No, everything will remain the same. You

will depart a little from what you are, but you will return. Everything will be fine. And in a short time, we will be walking through these same places once again. Life is an act that repeats itself."

"I hope so. I hope everything turns out well. You know, sometimes I think we are indebted to this country. There are so many people who directly or indirectly have made sacrifices for the good of others. But, what about us? What have we done? Now that I am, what we could say, closer to death, I ask myself these questions, what have we done, and what could we do for this piece of land that saw us come to life?"

"Your reasoning is good, but I must remind you of some things. First, being close to death is something that concerns all of us. We are all one step away from death. Nobody knows how or when he or she is going to die. The second thing is that this idea that we have not helped at all is not entirely true. There are many ways in which, without realizing it, we participate in the process of changing things. I, for example, know that I make a contribution through what I teach in school. As for you, I think that the mere fact of being alive, being a witness to the unfolding of time is enough for now. I know your chance will arrive. It's all a matter of waiting. For now, I am very happy to know that you are a conscious being. And let me say this, those who owe to the people are the ones who said they would be there for them but at the end were not. Those who fought the system and then, inexplicably, allowed themselves to be corrupted by it... Wait, Fernando, don't you think it's time to go to the airport?"

"Yes, I think so. With all these damn security check-points, better to get there early."

"Come on, then; lest things turn out as they did in Cenoví. Remember? We had to wait over an hour to cross the road because Victorio's caravan was passing."

"I remember. Everything is so different now! What was red yesterday, today is white; and those who ran from the guard are now protected by it. What a shame!

"That's right, the interesting thing about all this is that, not only are those in power swapped, but by swapping them, through some mechanism that occurs naturally, the ideas and perceptions of those around them are also altered. For example, Victorio used to say, and this was in his youth, when he wandered through the mountains, more scared than a goat, that the system oppressed us, for they allowed the empire to take all of our wealth. He said that we had to prevent it, and give the people what belonged to them. He said we had to fight to be free, and a lot of other stuff I cannot remember. Now, however, he fights to run the system, and says that the military are of and must belong to the people, to defend the people. He calls them brothers and asks them to be brothers to one another."

"*Coño*, but that's very good! I mean, it sounds good."

"You just said it, 'it sounds good,' but it is not. It's just talk."

"Well, whatever. It does sound good! Besides, after everything that happened to him, what would you have him talk about? That was some military camp he went through! They did a real number on that man! People say neither friends in high places nor the prayers of his mother were of any use. When they got him, they beat him up right then and there. And if that was in front of everybody, just imagine what they did to him once locked up. They just took him and nobody heard another word about it. Nothing was known until he reappeared on his own; and the shock of seeing him alive almost killed his mother: a mixture of fear, sadness and joy."

"Luis did not have it easy, either. But, as soon as he recovered, he returned to the fray. Stuck to his beliefs."

"Yeah, but there are not many men like Luis out there. Look how he ended, though, stuck in one of the containers in the *Regina;* and how he ruined Leonides's life. What could have been a good thing, see, nothing remains, not even the good wishes; and all that for going around voicing his Communist ideas; and all the running, from here to there, aimlessly, wasting his time. Sadly, all those who set his mind on fire with the Communist crap, not one showed up for him. Not one remembers him."

"You may be right," I said.

Then, we walked across the wooden bridge toward the exit. Behind us, in one of those presents that memories hide, we slowly moved away from the fresh breeze of the Caribbean Sea, the wine, and the flight of the swallows.

The End.

Rafael Antonio Tejada, Dominican storyteller, poet, and teacher, earned a degree in Agricultural Engineering from UASD University.

He was a member of the prestigious César Vallejo Literary Workshop (1987-1989) and has published *La sed del metal* (*The Thirst of Metal* -Short stories, 2012), *Tratado de ausencias / A Treatise on Absence* (Bilingual Poetry, 2021), and *La vida y los tiempos* (Spanish Novel, 2015) —winner of an accessit at the Federico García Godoy Funglode Awards / GFDD 2014.

Tejada has been invited to numerous literary events and book fairs, and featured in several anthologies. He is widely regarded as one of the foremost poets of the Dominican Diaspora in New York.

Index

Other books by the author:

La sed del metal
Spanish Short Stories

La vida y los tiempos
Spanish Novel

Tratado de ausencias / A Treatise on Absence
Bilingual Poetry

This book was completed in the month of August 2024, in the city of Roanoke, Texas, under the editorial supervision of Books&Smith.